This book belongs to

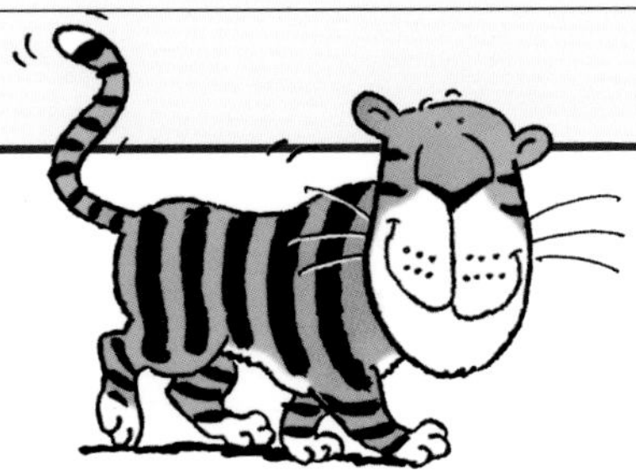

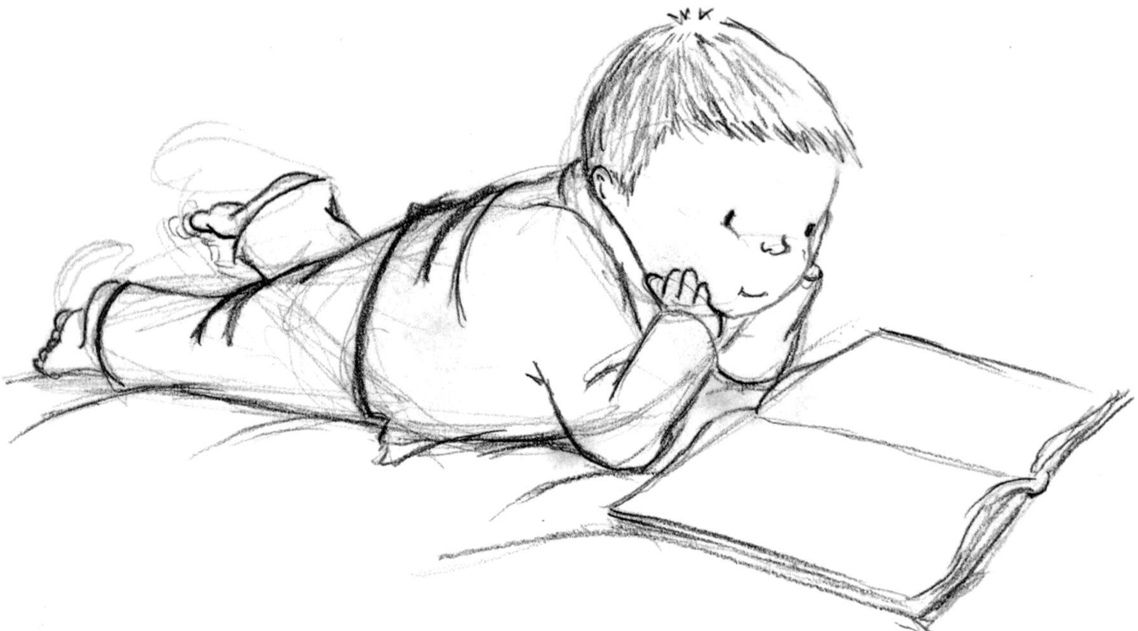

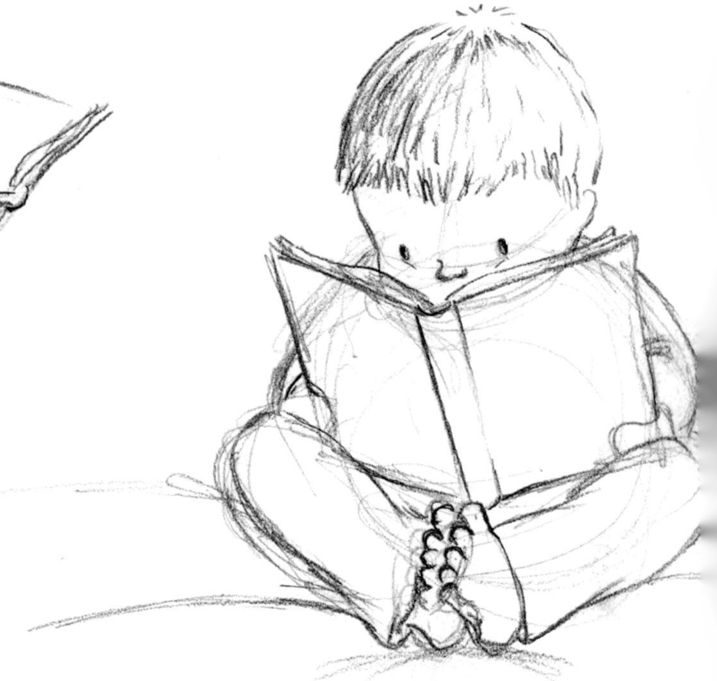

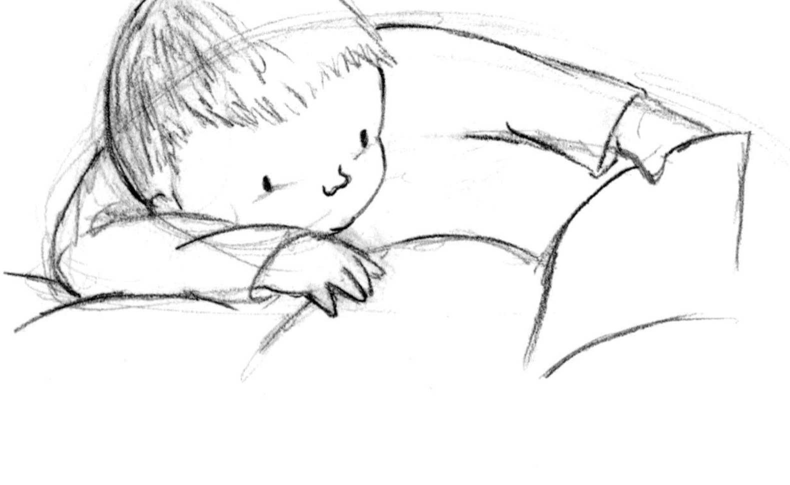

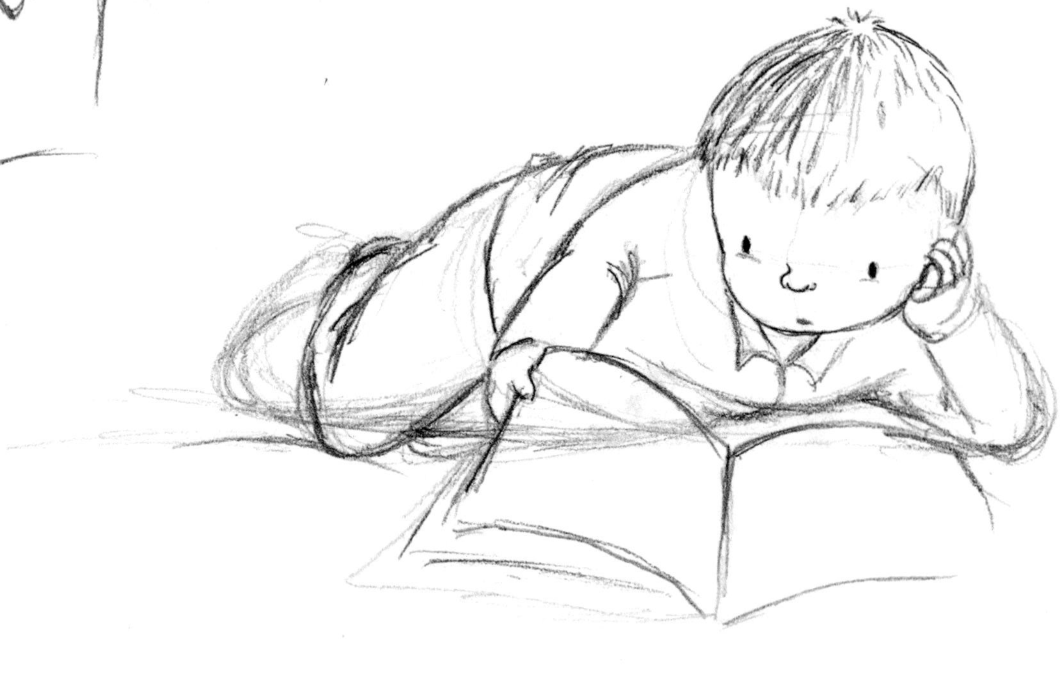

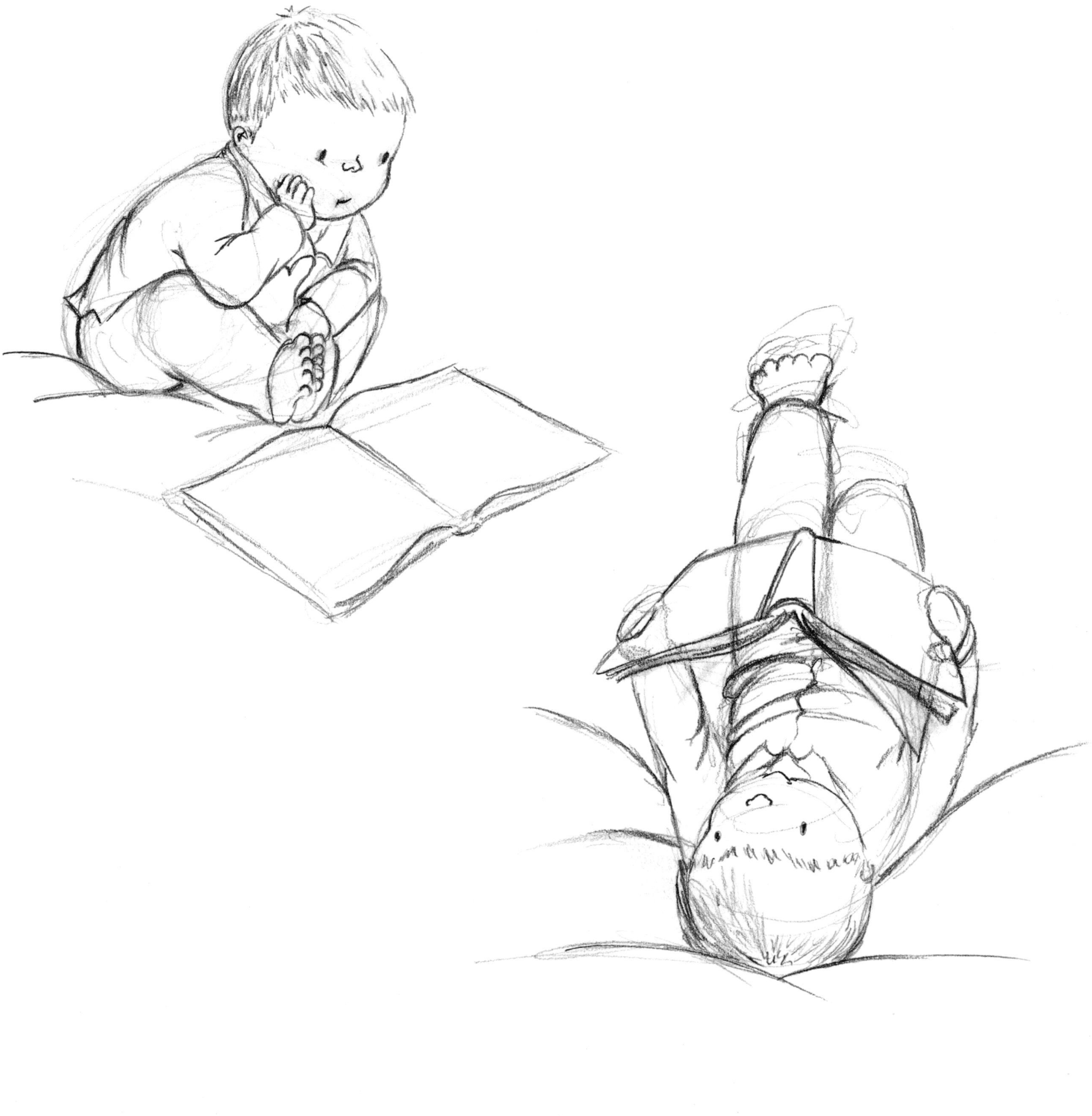

For Patrick
–N.Q.

For Mathias
–S.B.

tiger tales
an imprint of ME Media, LLC
202 Old Ridgefield Road, Wilton, CT 06897
Published in the United States 2005
Originally published as *Mama Beer* in Belgium 2004
By Uitgeverij Clavis, Amsterdam–Hasselt
Copyright © Uitgeverij Clavis, Amsterdam–Hasselt
CIP data is available
ISBN 1-58925-394-9
Printed in China

MAMA BEAR

by Natalie Quintart   Illustrated by Stéphanie Blanchart

tiger tales

Thomas hated to go to bed.

His mommy had already told him to go to bed one, two, three times. But Thomas's light was still on.

"I don't want to go to bed!" Thomas said. "My eyes haven't even started to itch yet." His eyes always itched when he was sleepy.

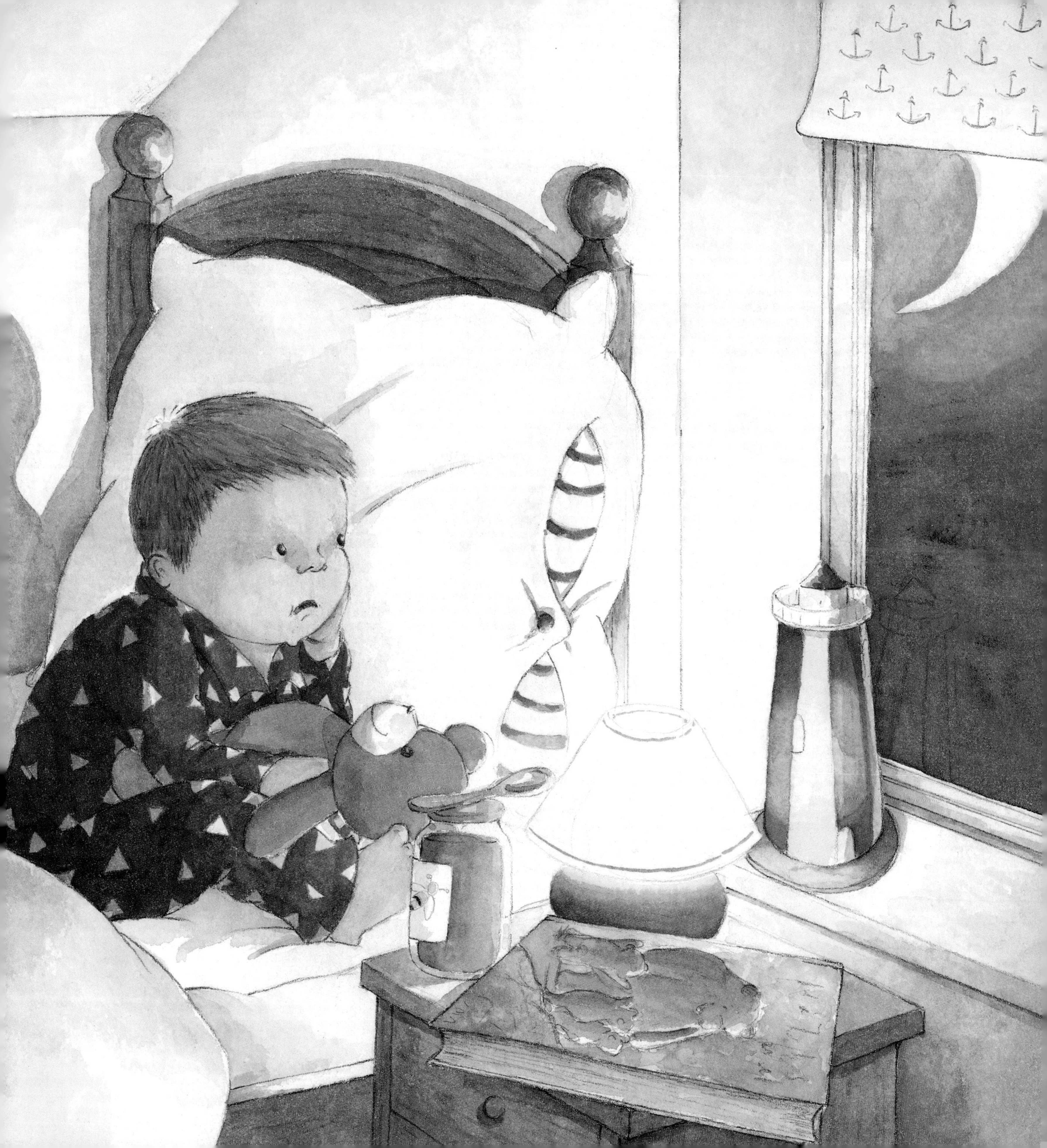

"Thomas, for the last time, you have to go to bed now," his mommy said. "And don't forget the spoonful of honey for your cough."

"Mommy, could you read me the story of Mama Bear again?" Thomas asked.

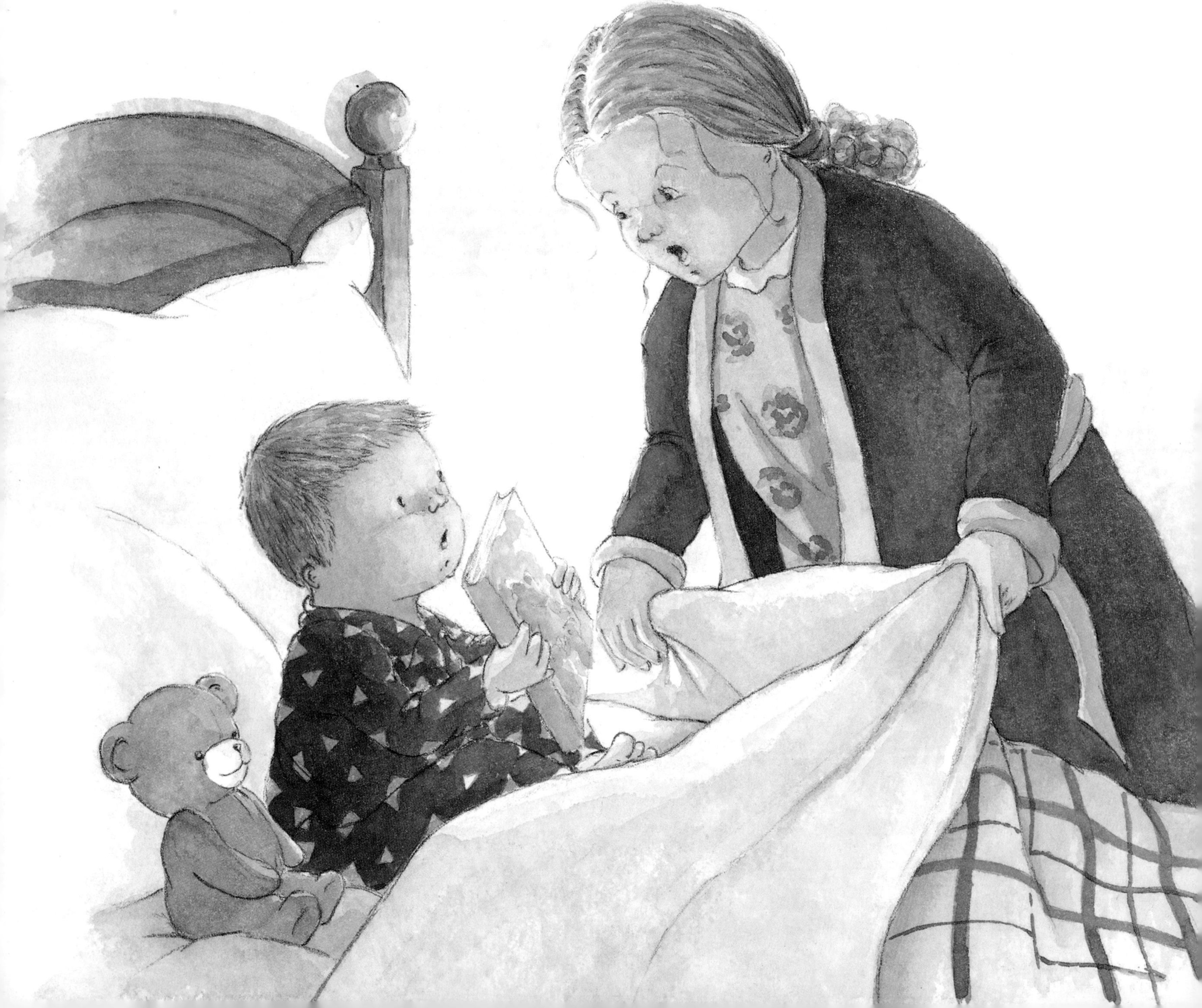

As she did every night, Thomas's mommy opened the book with a sigh. "Oh, how I'd love to be Mama Bear," she said. "Sleeping all winter and waking up again in the springtime."

Then she began to read:

Once there was a Mama Bear with three little bears who never wanted to go to bed. Instead of hibernating like other bears, they played and fussed and fought....

And as she did every night, Thomas's mommy was the first to fall asleep.

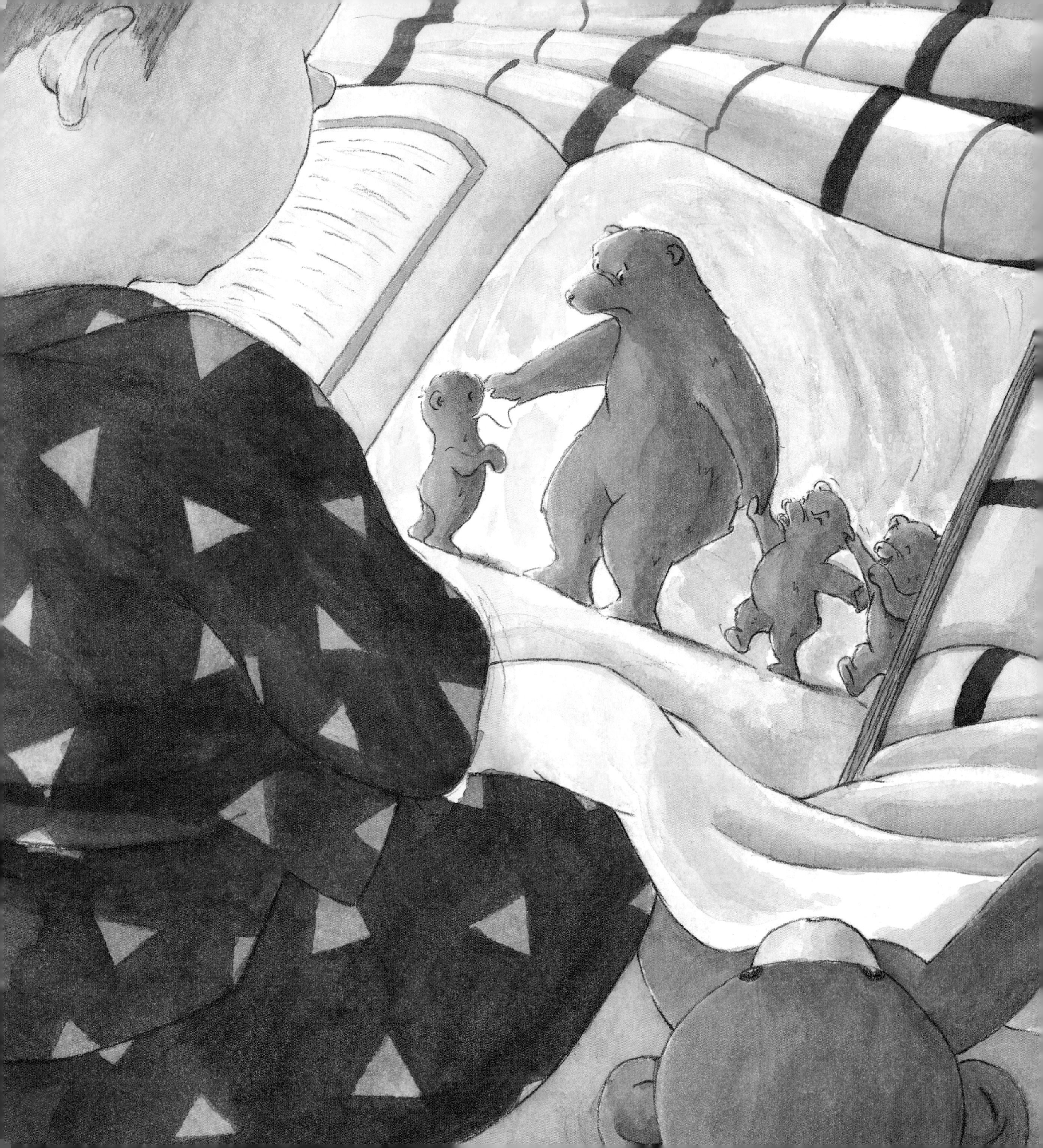

So Thomas looked at the book by himself.

The little bears were awake again, and causing trouble!

They were growling—loudly!

They were hungry. . . .

"Oh, there's such a delicious smell out there!" said Mama Bear. And she jumped . . .

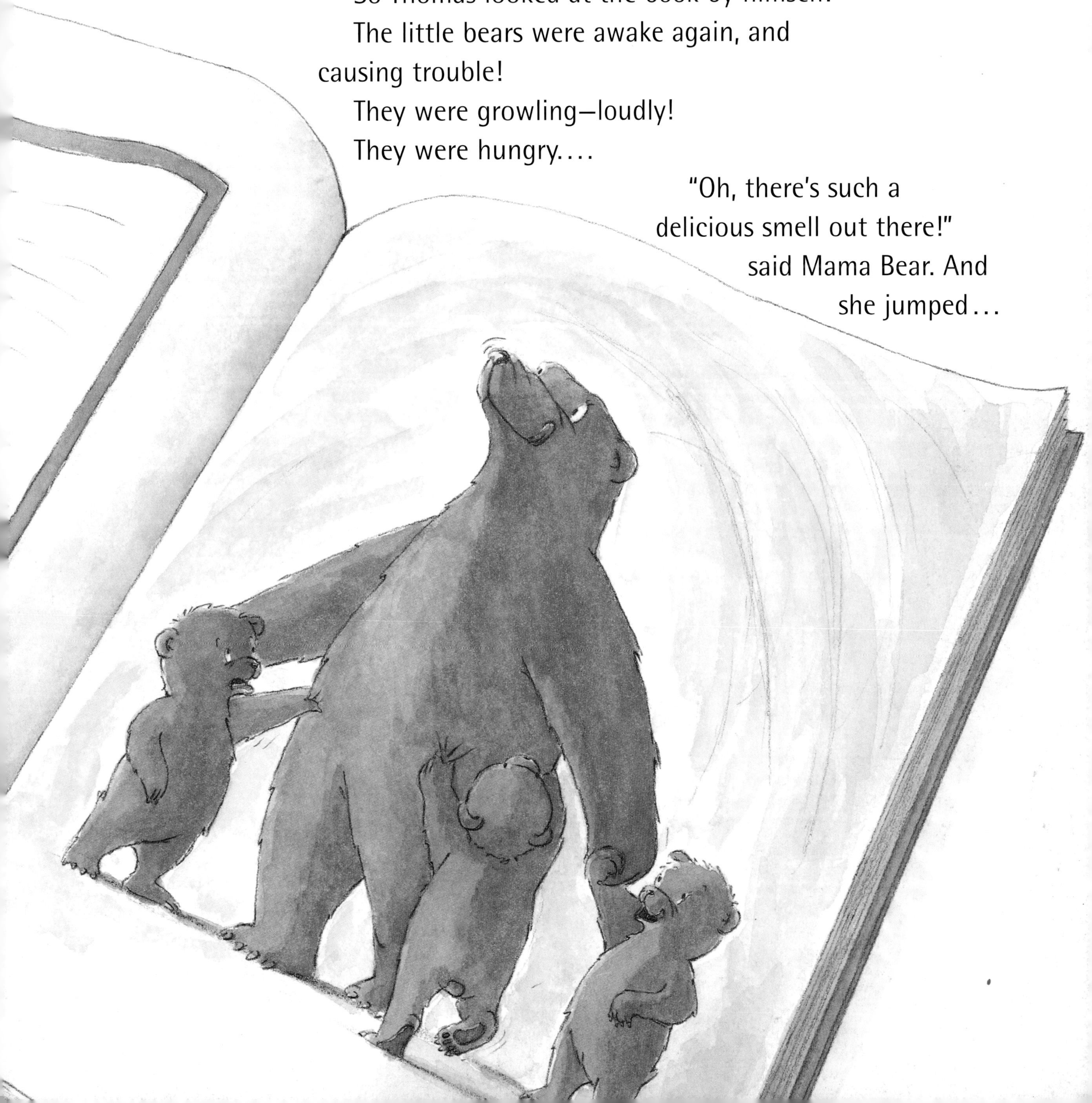

right into Thomas's bed!

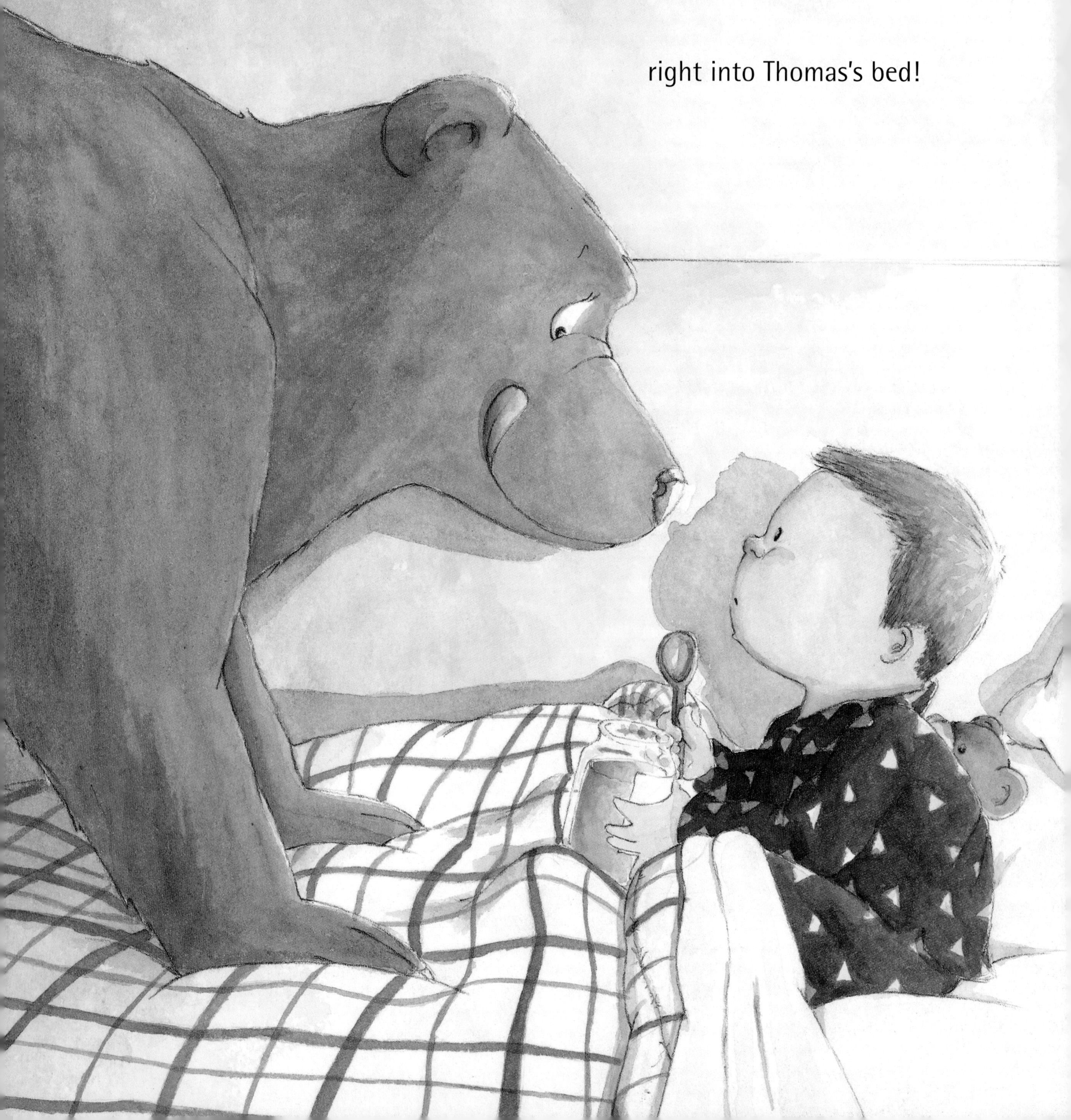

"Help, Mommy! There's a bear in my room!" Thomas cried.

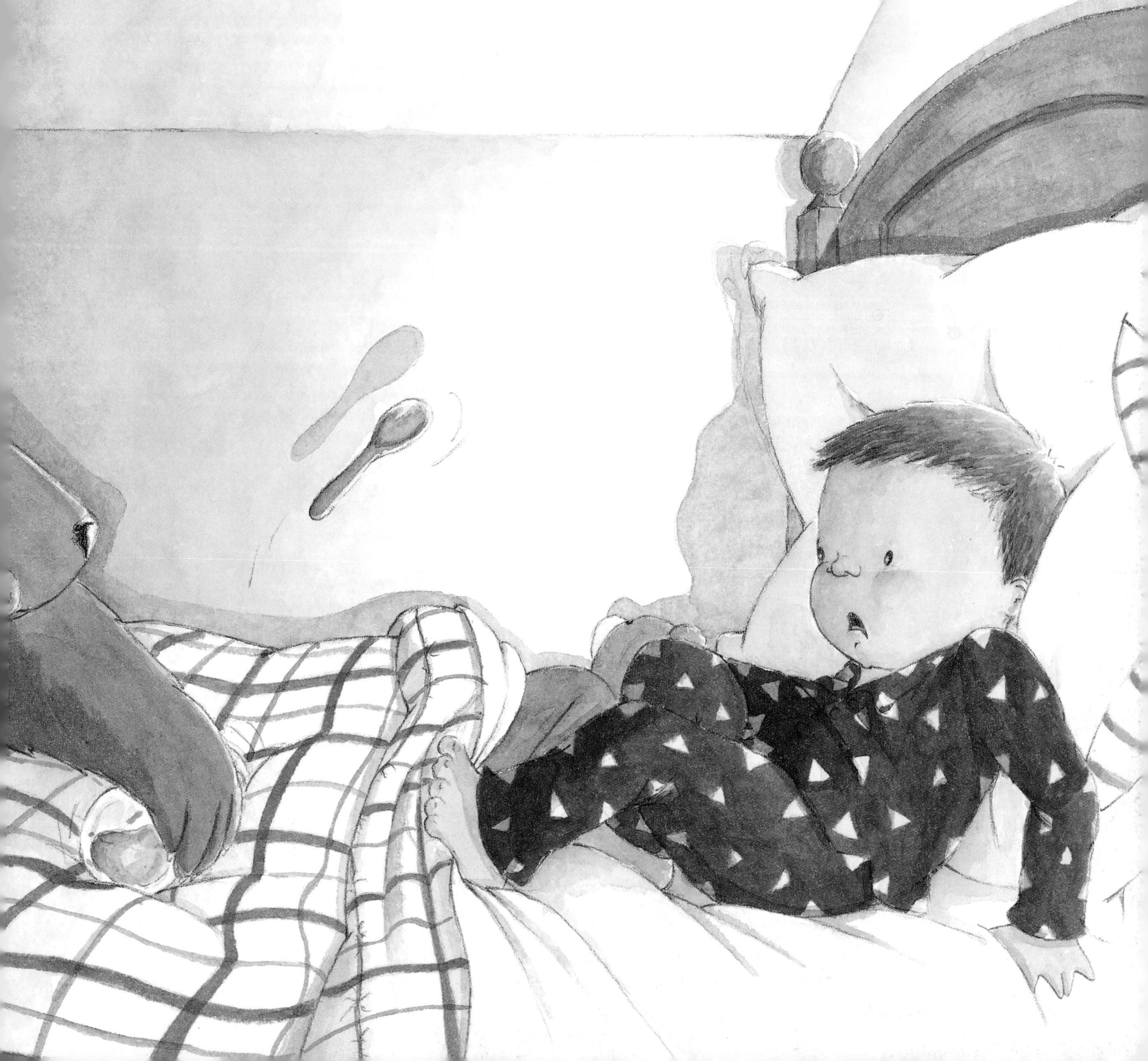

"It's me, Mama Bear!" she said. "Look! I've traded places with your mommy so she could rest in my cave. That's what she wanted, wasn't it?"

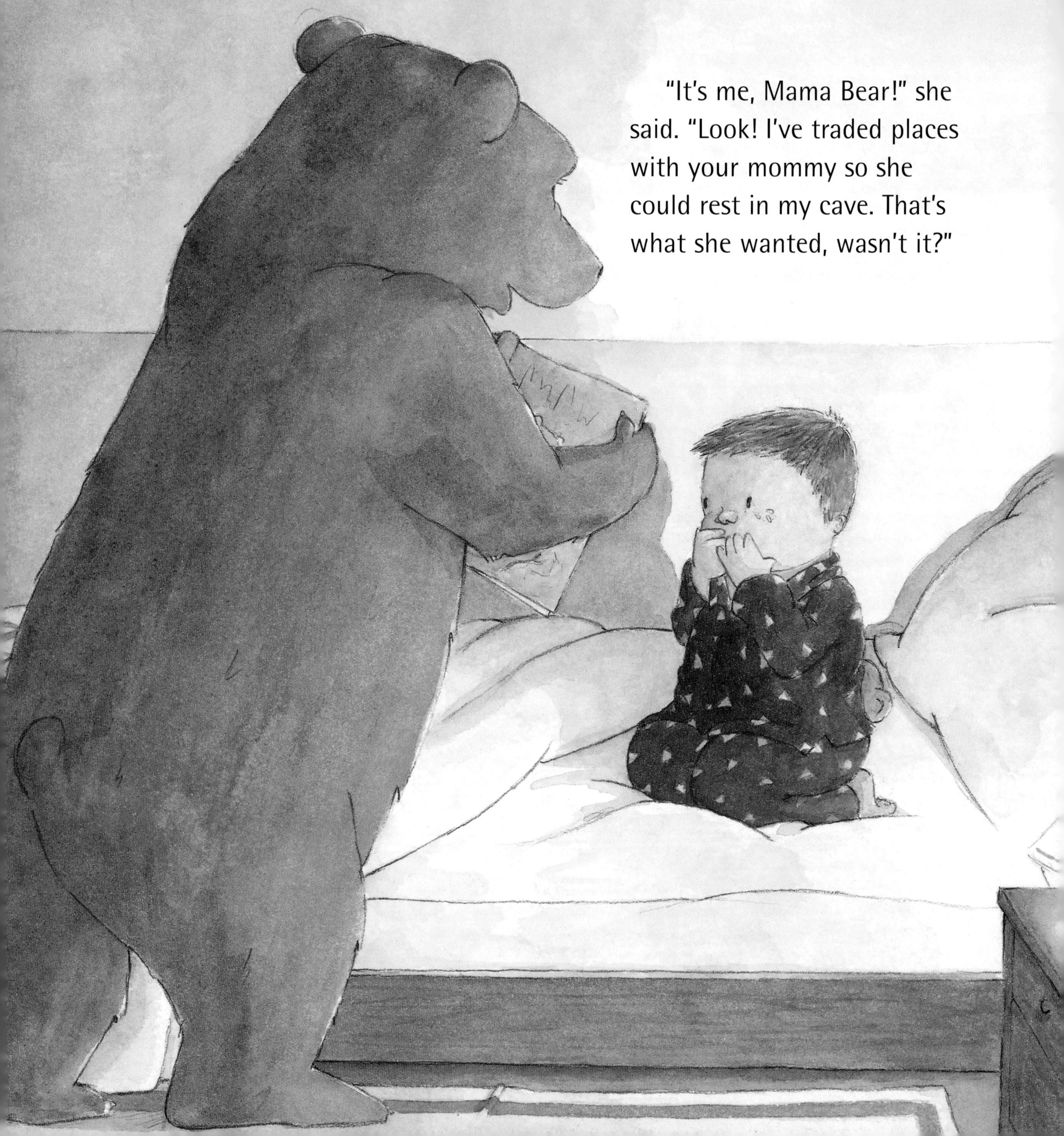

"See how peacefully she's lying there? Let's let her sleep a little while longer."

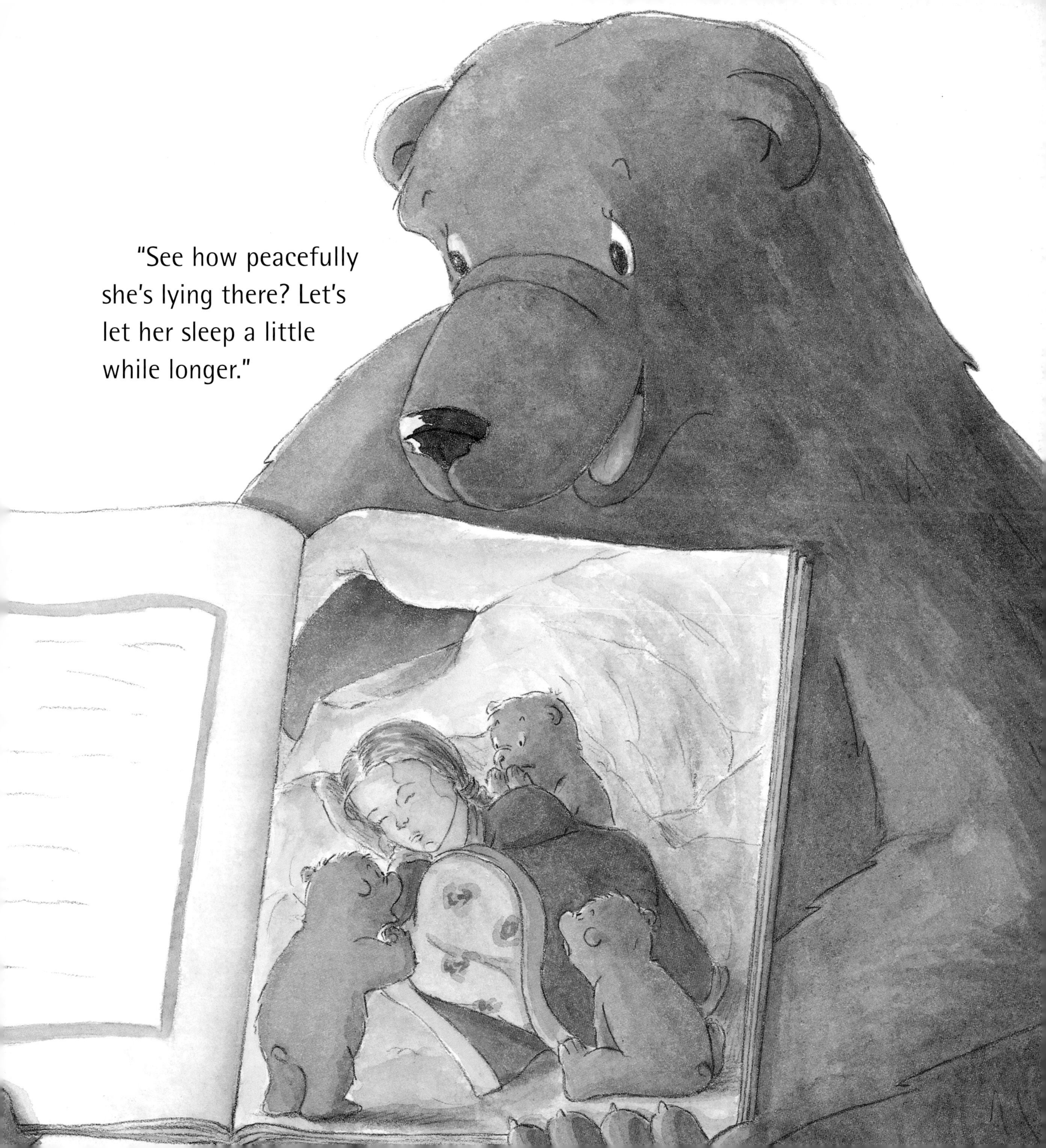

"Now, time to see what smells so good! I need food for my little bears.

"I'll grab just a few things!" she called to Thomas.

Mama Bear grabbed the cereal, nuts, apples, potato chips, pretzels, cookies, a jar of honey, cheese, another jar of honey, a few more things…

and a loaf of bread.

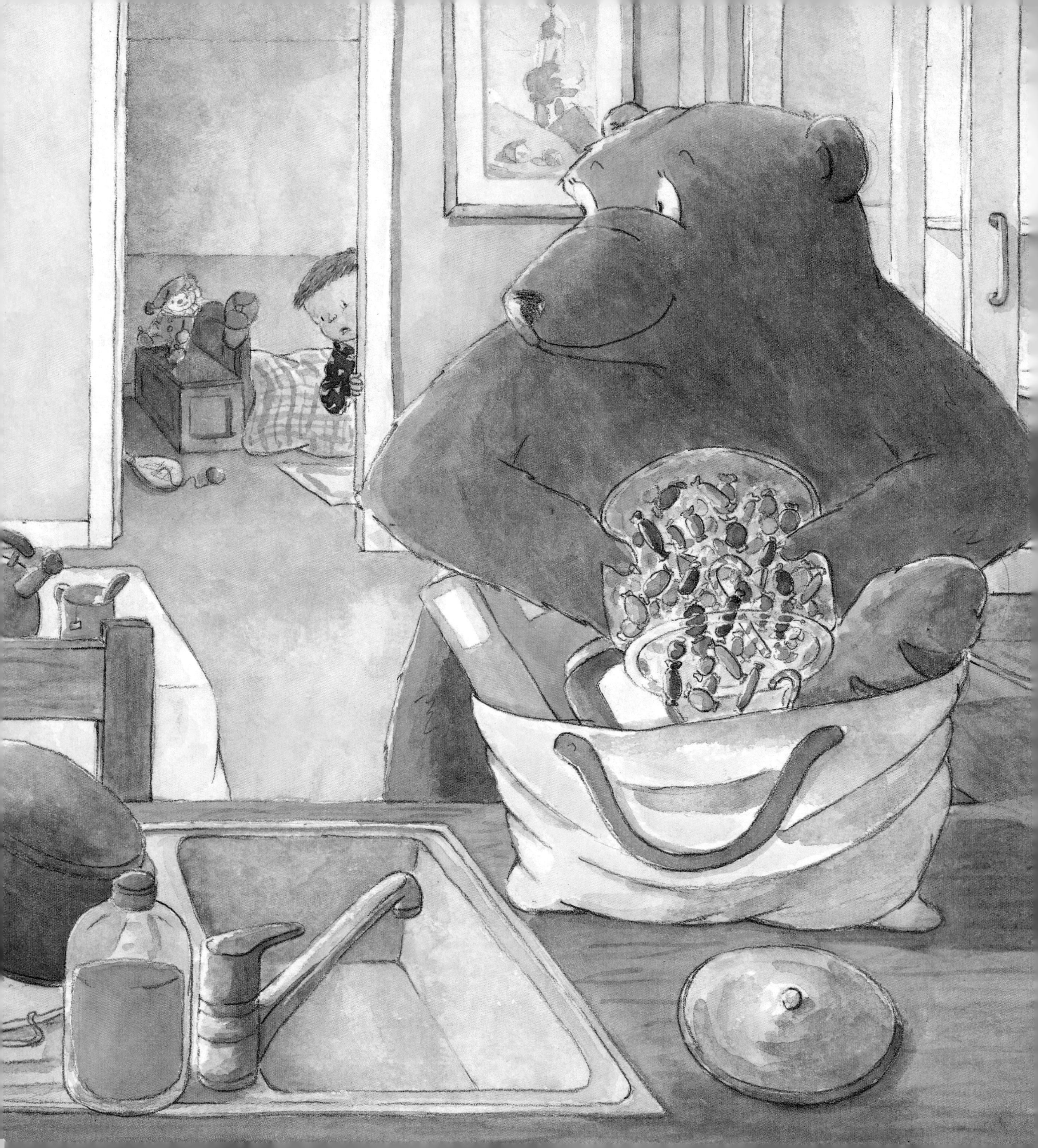

"Mommy, wake up!"
Thomas said. "Don't
leave me alone with
that crazy bear!"

"Don't worry, Thomas. I'm
going back to my cave now,"
said Mama Bear.

"Um, Thomas's mommy?" Mama Bear called. "Could you please swap places with me again?"

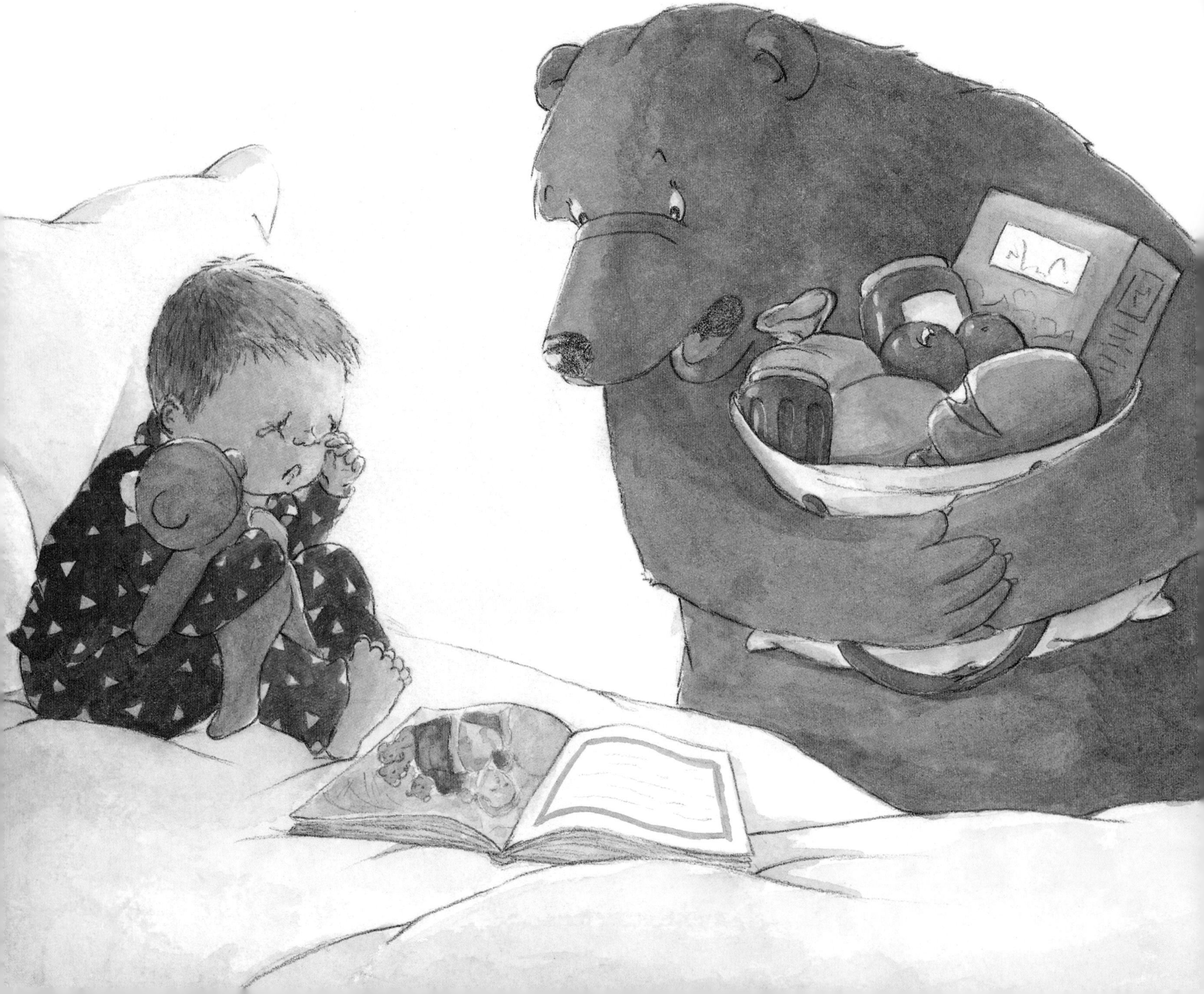

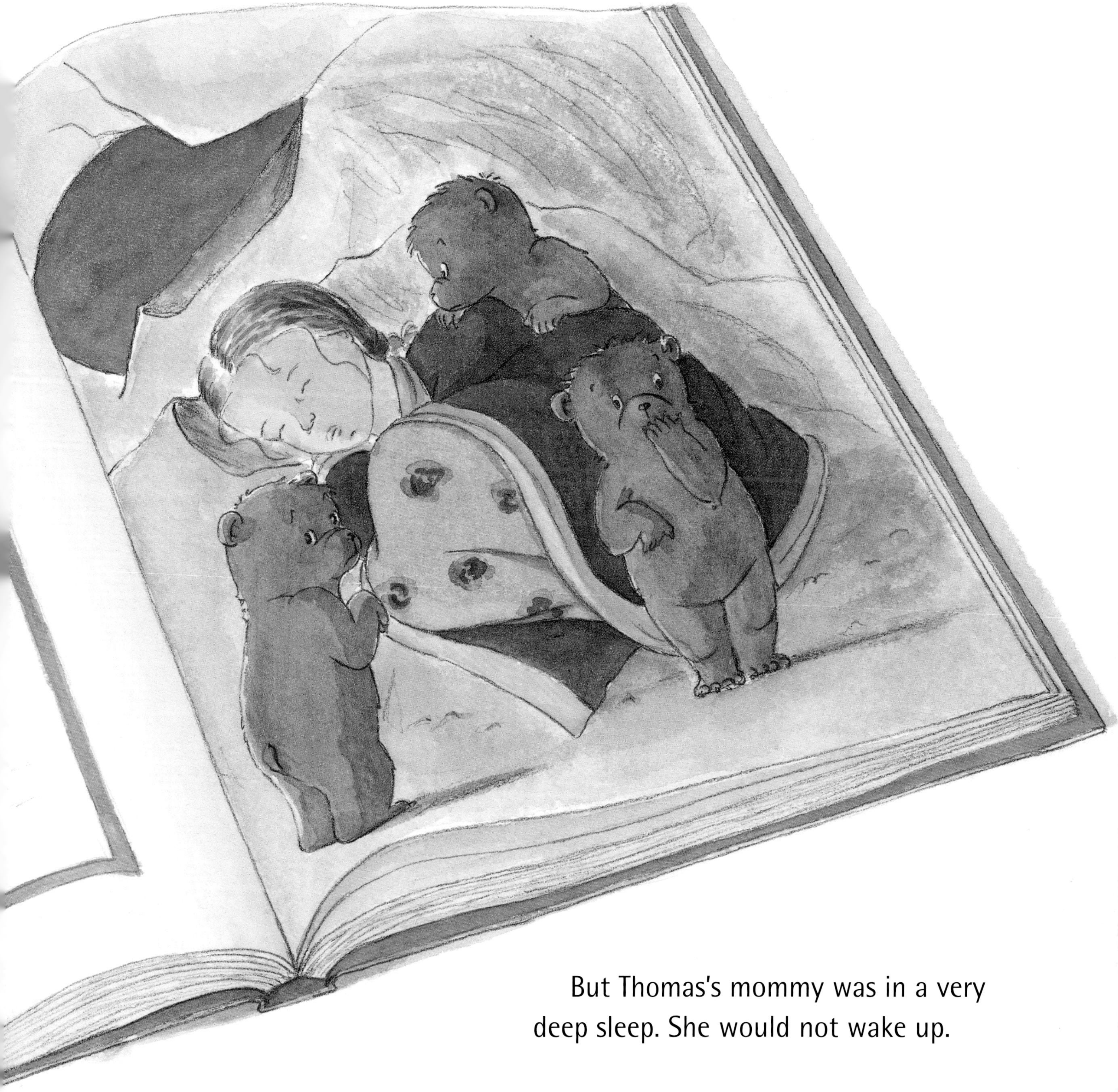

But Thomas's mommy was in a very deep sleep. She would not wake up.

Mama Bear tried blowing
on the book.

She shook the pages as
hard as she could.
"Come on out, Thomas's
mommy!" she said.

Desperate...

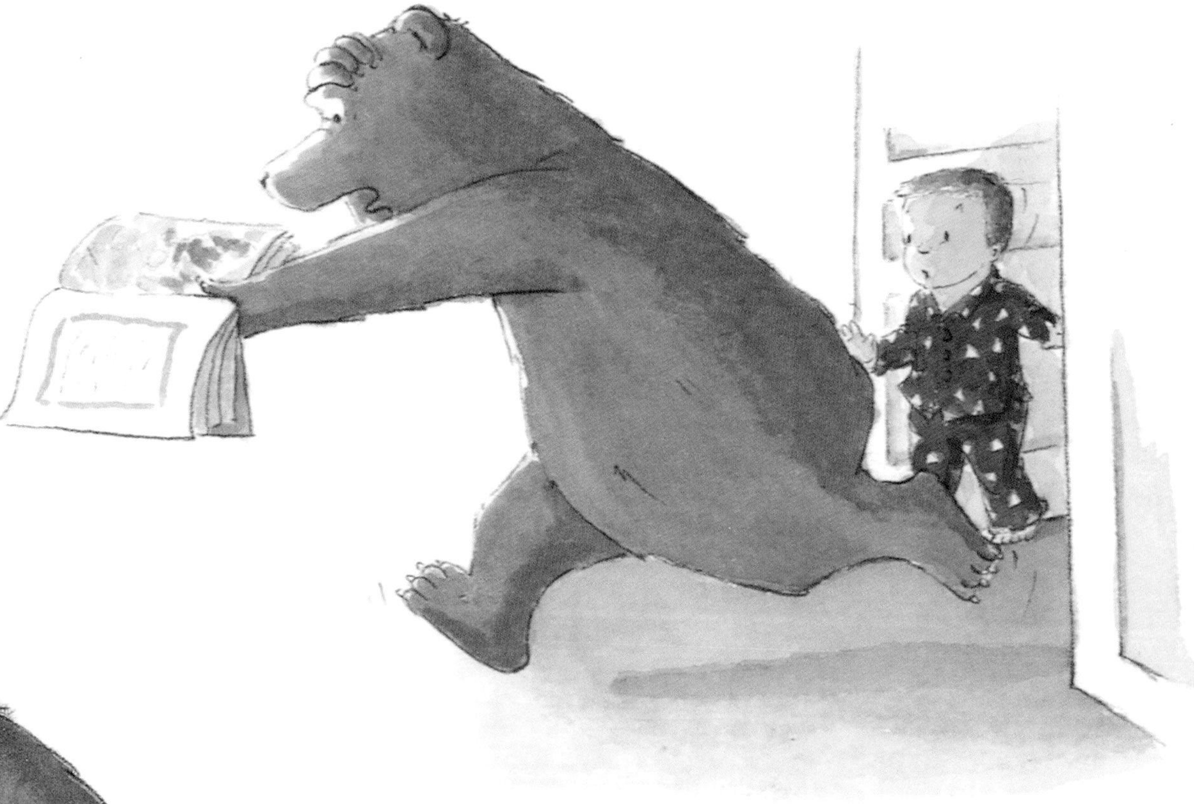

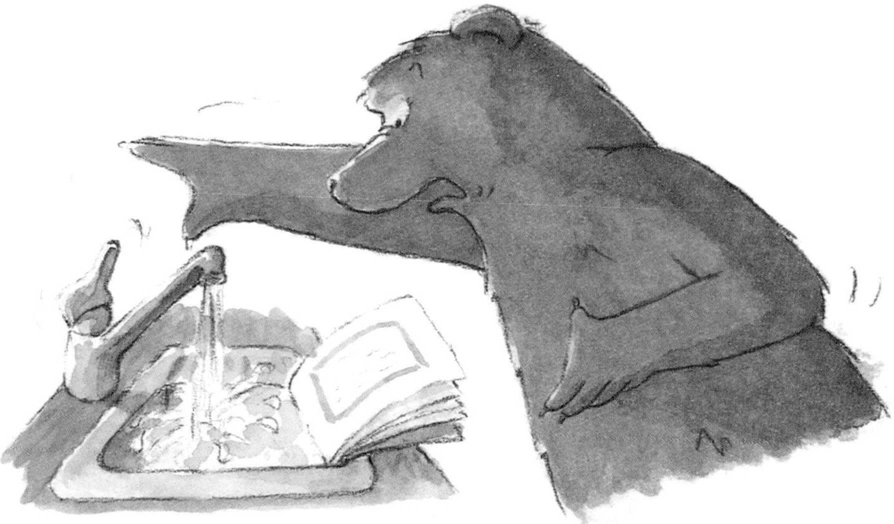

Mama Bear dropped the book into icy cold water.

But nothing worked.

"Dear me, Thomas! I'm afraid your mommy won't wake up until spring!"

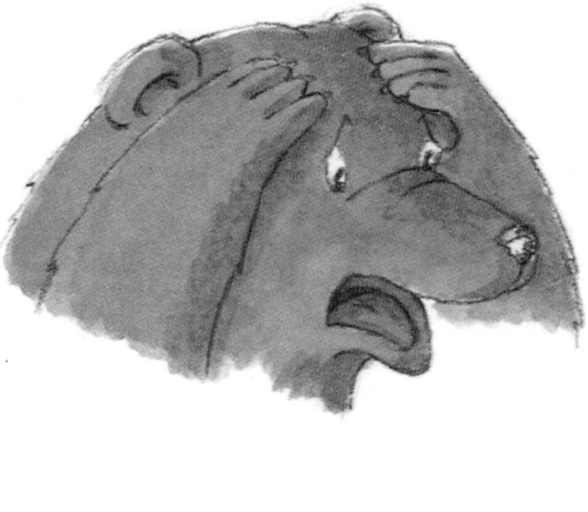

Thomas was worried.

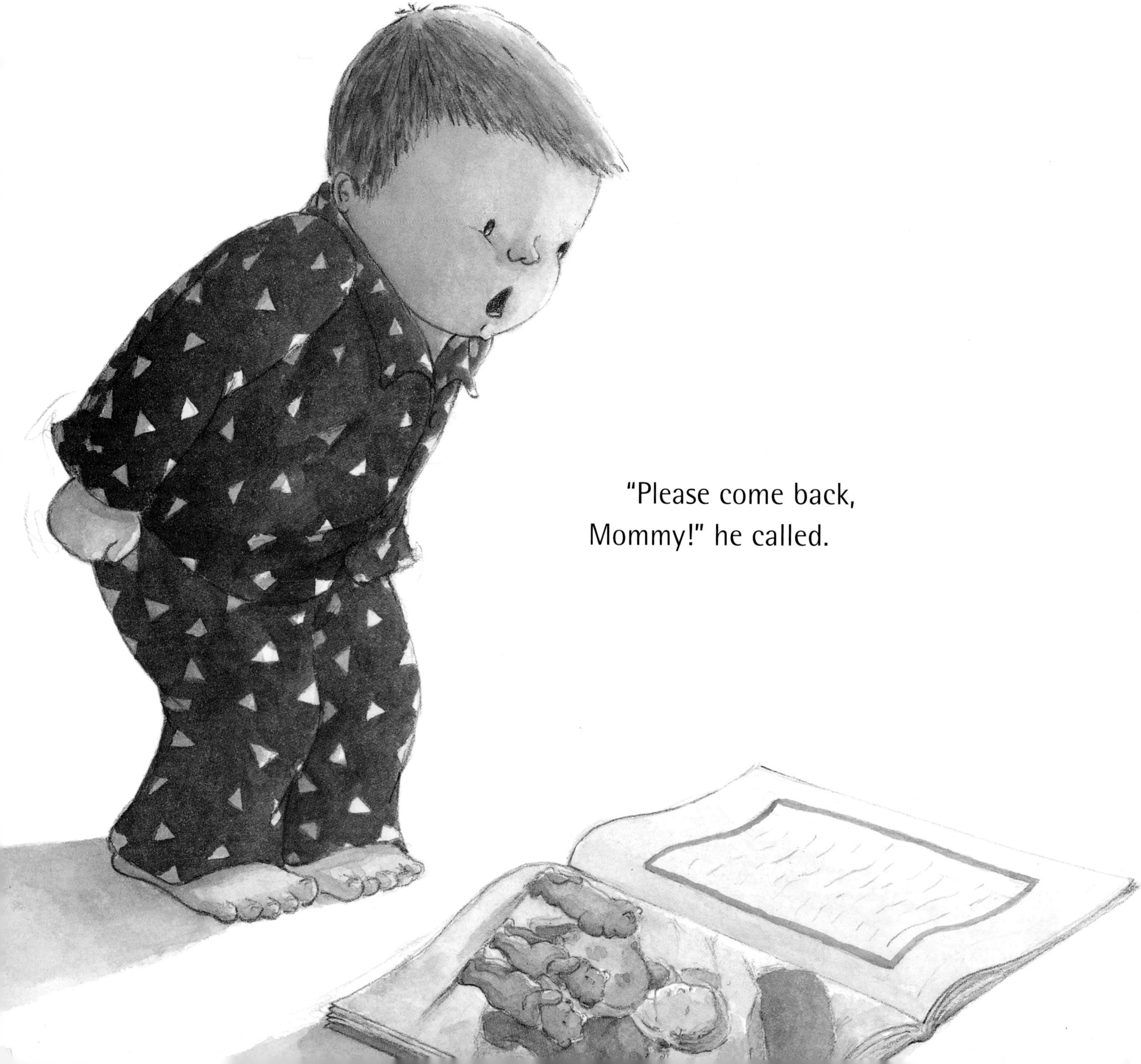

"Please come back, Mommy!" he called.

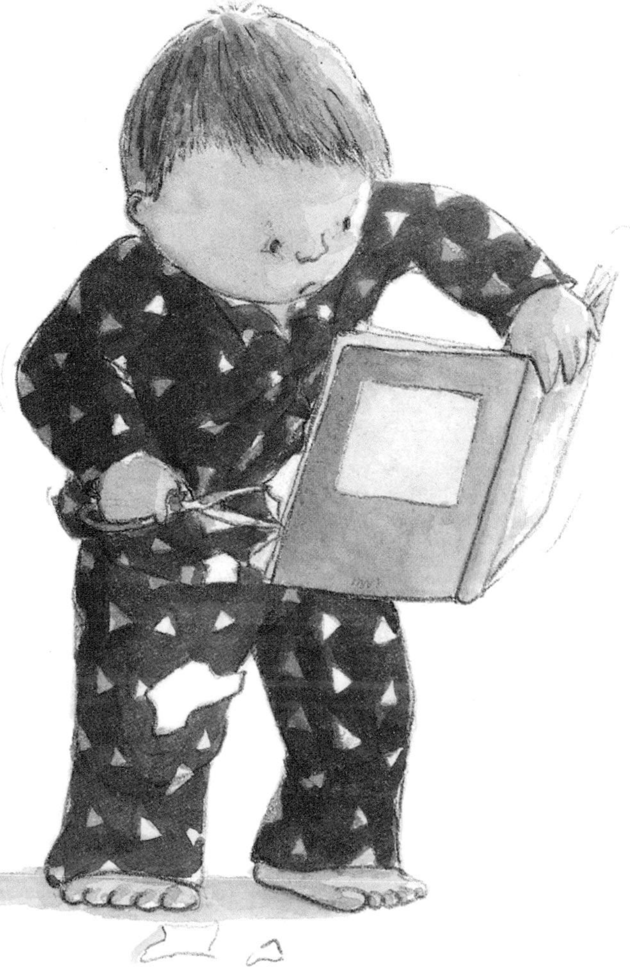

Finally, he had an idea! Thomas got a pair of scissors and tried to cut his mommy out of the book.

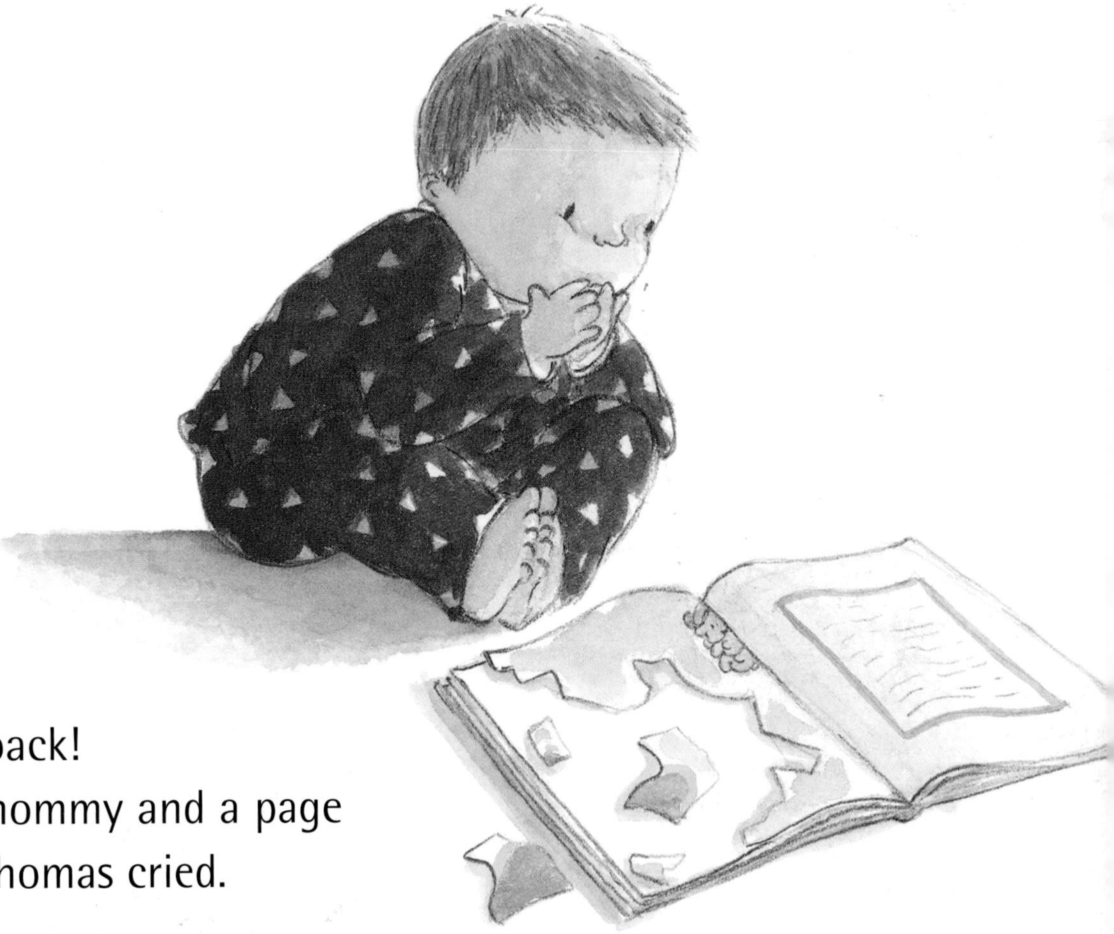

But she did not come back!

"Now I'm missing my mommy and a page from my favorite book!" Thomas cried.

"Mama Bear, is my mommy so tired because of me? I can be big trouble. Especially at bedtime."

"Don't be silly," she said. "It's my fault. I should have never left home. I miss my boys! Even though they can be HUGE trouble."

"Do you still think they're good bears?" Thomas asked.

"The best in the whole wide world," said Mama Bear.

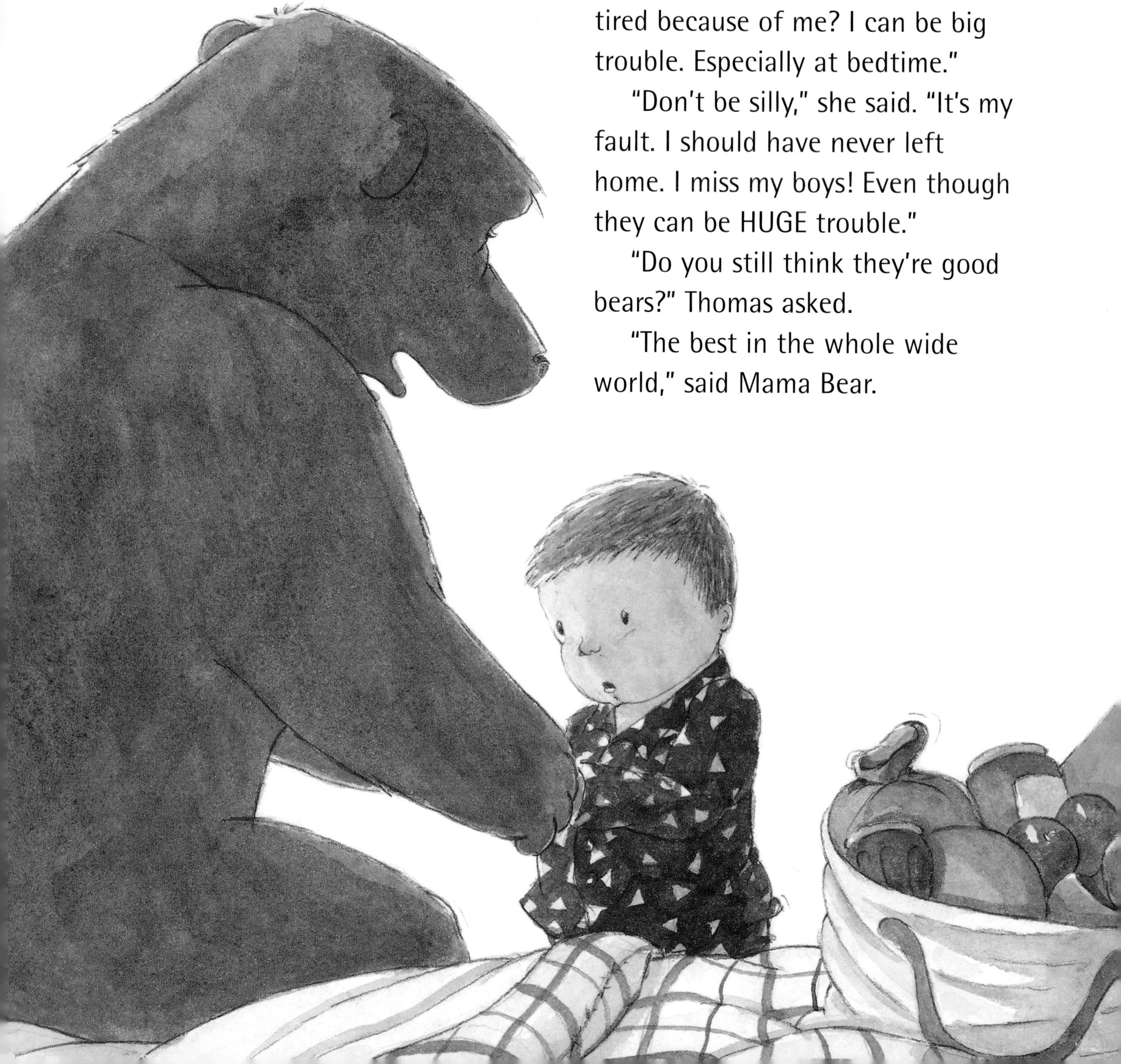

Thomas found his crayons.
He made a new page for his book.

"Look, Mama Bear! This is my
mommy. She's awake and ready
to come home!"

At last, Thomas's eyes began to itch. He snuggled up to Mama Bear's fur and, in an instant, they both fell asleep.

Until…

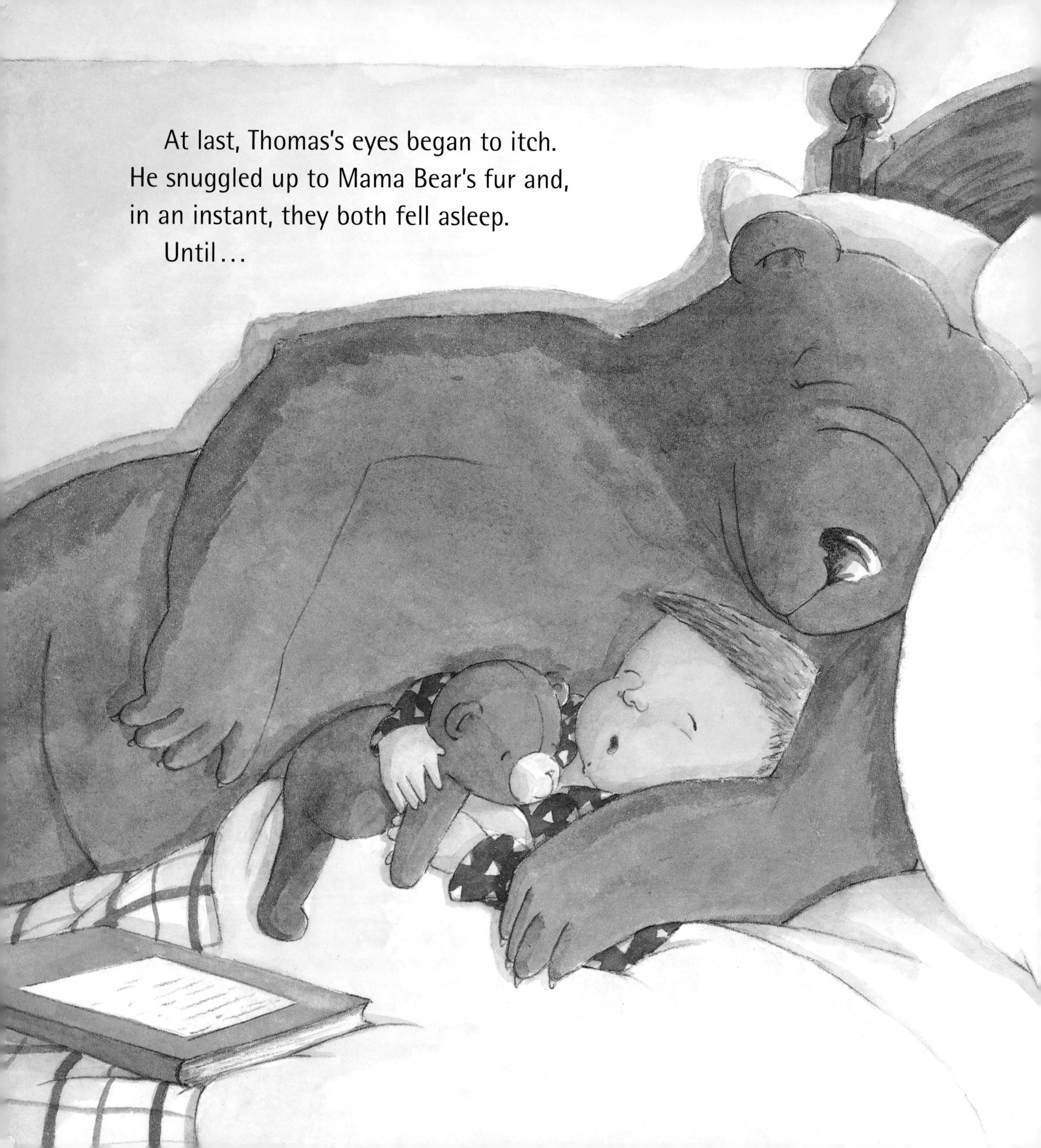

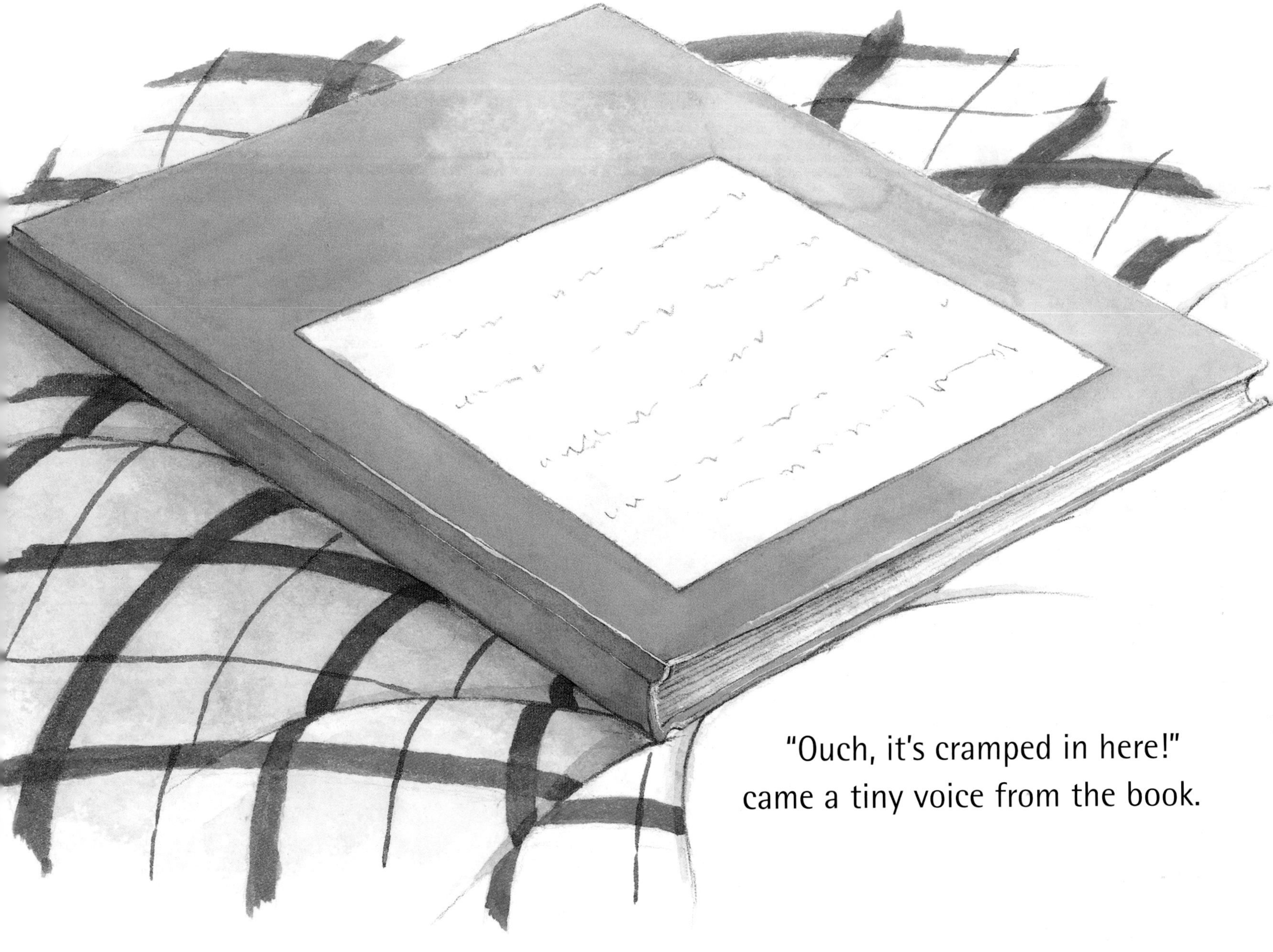

"Ouch, it's cramped in here!"
came a tiny voice from the book.

"I feel like I've been sleeping all winter long!" Thomas's mommy said with a stretch.

"How did you sleep, Thomas?"

"Mommy! I'm so happy to see you!"

"You are the best mommy in the whole wide world!" Thomas cried.

"And you, Thomas," his mommy said, hugging him tightly, "are the very best boy!"

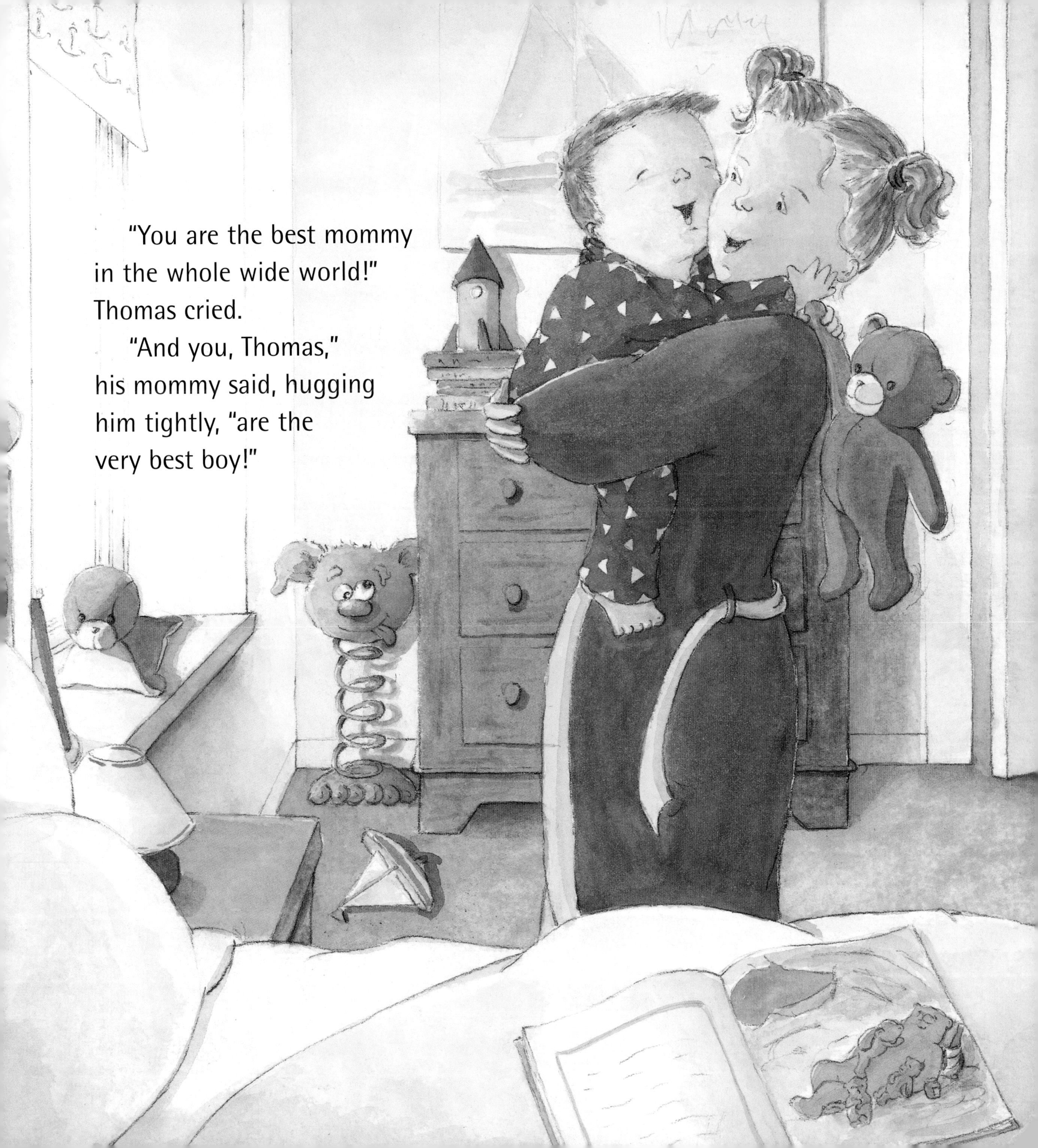

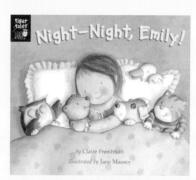

Night-Night, Emily!
by Claire Freedman
Illustrated by Jane Massey

Night-Night, Emily!
by Claire Freedman
illustrated by Jane Massey
ISBN 1-58925-390-6

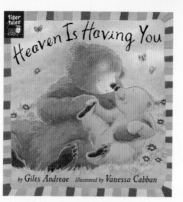

Heaven Is Having You
by Giles Andreae
Illustrated by Vanessa Cabban

Heaven Is Having You
by Giles Andreae
illustrated by Vanessa Cabban
ISBN 1-58925-388-4

The Very Lazy Ladybug
Isobel Finn & Jack Tickle

The Very Lazy Ladybug
by Isobel Finn
illustrated by Jack Tickle
ISBN 1-58925-379-5

Explore the world of tiger tales!

More fun-filled and exciting stories await you!
Look for these titles and more at your local library or bookstore.
And have fun reading!

tiger tales
202 Old Ridgefield Road, Wilton, CT 06897

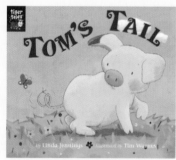

TOM'S TAIL
by Linda Jennings
illustrated by Tim Warnes

Tom's Tail
by Linda Jennings
illustrated by Tim Warnes
ISBN 1-58925-383-3

WHEN PIGS FLY!
by Stefan Boonen
Illustrated by Loufane

When Pigs Fly!
by Stefan Boonen
Illustrated by Loufane
ISBN 1-58925-384-1

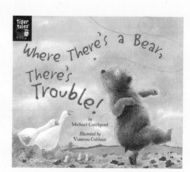

Where There's a Bear, There's Trouble!
by Michael Catchpool
Illustrated by Vanessa Cabban

Where There's a Bear, There's Trouble!
by Michael Catchpool
illustrated by Vanessa Cabban
ISBN 1-58925-389-2

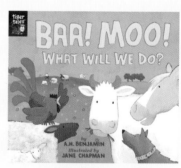

BAA! MOO! WHAT WILL WE DO?
by A.H. BENJAMIN
Illustrated by JANE CHAPMAN

Baa! Moo! What Will We Do?
by A.H. Benjamin
illustrated by Jane Chapman
ISBN 1-58925-381-7